CHILLY BOLLY GUACAMOLLY
text: 2007 GABRIELA ZORRILLA
illustrations 2007 SANDRA SERRANO
All rights reserved

Summary: Chilly Bolly, a Mexican tomato, prepares the most
delicious guacamole ever. He and his
best friend, Miss Cebolla, plan on selling guacamole to buy
a wheelchair for their friend Doña Zucchini.
However, the Rancho where they live, gets
hit by a draught and Chilly Bolly and Miss Cebolla have
to rely on their friends to survive.
ISBN: 978-1-60585-601-8 (hardcover)

Price: $16.95

1. Mexican Tomato-Fiction
Text copyright 2008 by Gabriela Zorrilla.
Published in 2008 by Don Papel Editorial. Cuernavaca, Morelos
Printed by Dicograf, Cuernavaca, Mor., MEXICO.
Edited by Don Papel
Book design by María Isabel Zorrilla.
For more information e-mail the author gzorrilla@mac.com

-A Chacho, mi esposo, por ser la razón de mi vida; y a mis hijas Andrea, Jimena y Ana Paula, mi inspiración. G.Z.

-A Neri, mi editora, por confiar en mí. G.Z.

Chilly Bolly Guacamolly

by Gabriela Zorrilla

Illustrated by: Sandra Serrano

Chilly Bolly tried to hold his hand steady on his old guitar. He didn't want to look nervous to Doña Zucchini, but he truly was. "How can I make her believe that a tomato like me can prepare the best *guacamole*...?"

For years, Doña Zucchini had had a *guacamole* stand at her *Rancho*. But now she was very sick and she was looking for a chef who could keep making the famous *guacamole*. She was not sure she really needed a tomato; nevertheless, she decided to call Chilly Bolly and give him a chance. It took her just five seconds after she dipped her *tortilla* into his *guacamole* to hire him.

"You know how to prepare *guacamole* just like I do," said happily the sweet old woman. "Please Chilly Bolly, come to the *Rancho* to help me prepare the *guacamole*".

Chilly Bolly was a very red, a very chubby and a very Mexican chef. He was a perfectly round tomato with a funny big black moustache, two cowboy boots and a perfect sparkling white smile. He was so happy to go live at the *Rancho* with Doña Zucchini. Her *Rancho* was beautiful, full of green and exotic trees. It had a lake and a lot of shaded paths to walk on.

Every morning Chilly Bolly checked that the ingredients he needed were ready to be mixed. He had to be sure that the avocados were soft enough to be smashed, the fat onions almost crunchy, the huge tomatoes juicy and firm, the humongous *chiles* very *picantes* and the spicy *cilantro* fresh and crispy.

It was so extremely delicious that people from distant places wouldn't mind waiting in line for hours to buy lots of *guacamole* jars.

"Chilly Bolly," Doña Zucchini said sadly one day, "My legs really hurt so I have to go see a doctor who is very far from the *Rancho*. You and your best friend Miss Cebolla are the only ones who can help me take care of the plantation".

"*No se preocupe Doña*. Everything will be fine. I will prepare the *guacamole* and Miss Cebolla will take care of the stand," replied the tomato.

Chilly Bolly helped her pack her things. She looked so fragile, almost incapable of walking any more. Later that day, she left for the hospital.

Miss Cebolla was a firm and juicy off-white onion and Chilly Bolly's oldest friend. Before she met Chilly Bolly, she didn't have any other friends because, like all the onions do, she made everybody cry. The day she met him she couldn't believed he talked to her so enthusiastically for so long. She realized Chilly Bolly enjoyed being with her and he didn't mind shedding a few tears when they got together. She went to live with him at the *Rancho* and they became inseparable friends.

"*Querida amiga*," the tomato said to Miss Cebolla when Doña Zucchini left. "I need your help. We must double the *guacamole* sales. The doctors just told Doña Zucchini that she will not be able to walk anymore. We will save money and buy her a wheelchair!"

"But of course! We all love her so much! We must work hard until we can get it!" she answered.

Chilly Bolly, Miss Cebolla and everybody at the plantation worked long days and nights to sell double the amount of *guacamole*. For weeks they barely had time to sleep. But after months and months of hard work, they finally reached their goal.

"We did it *amigos*! We are a great team! We finally have enough money," said Chilly Bolly proudly, hugging everyone. "I will go get the wheelchair with the money we made, so Doña Zucchini can have it when she comes back from the hospital."

Weeks went by and Doña Zucchini still had not come back. The new wheelchair sat lonely in Doña Zucchini's room, waiting for her to return.

Summer arrived and the heat became unbearable. The draught had begun. The sun's rays had no mercy on the vegetables at the *Rancho* and there was not enough water for all.

Chilly Bolly felt helpless. He was so terribly sad to see all of his friends suffering. He cried and cried. He had no strength left to help his friends. Chilly Bolly tried his best to keep everybody alive but as the days passed, all the vegetables became more and more dehydrated. The tears kept coming out from his eyes. Suddenly he had an idea.

"*Se me ocurre algo* ! I need as many people as possible to come to the *Rancho* to see Miss Cebolla," Chilly Bolly thought, wiping away his tears. "If only I could move and go bring them," he sighed.

Finally, Doña Zucchini was able to leave the hospital and come back to the *Rancho*. When she opened the two big old doors, she could not believed her eyes. Everything at the *Rancho* was completely dry and there was no sign of life anywhere. All the plants laid motionless on the ground.

"Chilly Bolly! Miss Cebolla! Where are you?" Chilly Bolly heard Doña Zucchini calling in the distance. "PLEASE ANSWER ME! Somebody...PLEASE!"

She called for Chilly Bolly and all her friends for what seemed like hours, but there was no answer. Finally, she went to her room. She saw a new wheelchair with a huge red ribbon and a tag with her name on it. "They knew I really needed it," she thought thankfully. "I need to do something to save my friends". She got into her new wheelchair and went to town faster than ever. When she arrived, she realized the whole town was suffering from the draught as well.

"WHAT AM I GOING TO DO?" she cried.

Meanwhile at the *Rancho*, Chilly Bolly drank some drops of water he found in a puddle and started to feel better. He gained some strenght and decided to go ahead with his idea. He took Miss Cebolla into his arms and placed her at the *Rancho's* front door.

People from near towns heard about the problem at the *Rancho* and decided to go there to see what they could do to help poor Doña Zucchini. When everyone got there, they saw Miss Cebolla lying at the entrance and they started to cry. They cried for so many hours that their tears filled the ground like an unstoppable torrent. The lake that was dry because of the draught filled up with all the tears. Little by little the vegetables absorbed the water. Like magic, green plants grew from the wet ground.

"*Bravo*! My idea worked! Miss Cebolla made them cry!" Chilly Bolly thought excited.

"*Mi querida amiga,*" said Chilly Bolly to her friend "You have saved us. You made everybody cry and their tears became the water we needed."

For the first time ever, Miss Cebolla felt so proud of herself.

As time passed, the vegetables returned to their original fresh color. Thanks to the tears of thousands of people, the entire plantation recovered.

Chilly Bolly and Miss Cebolla greeted Doña Zucchini with a big smile.

"My precious friends, you are alive!" said Doña Zucchini joyfully. "This is the best moment of my life. *Gracias* Chilly Bolly! *Gracias* Miss Cebolla!"

The tomato and the onion jumped onto Doña Zucchini's lap and she hugged them with all her heart.

Chilly Bolly, Miss Cebolla and Doña Zucchini remained best friends forever and they continued preparing their delicious guacamole.

From that day on, everybody at the *Rancho* and around town called the tomato by a new name: CHILLY BOLLY GUACAMOLLY.

"I really like my new name," he said to Miss Cebolla, while a small tear rolled down his puffy cheek.

Chilly Bolly Guacamolly, the very red, very chubby, and very Mexican tomato held his old guitar again and smiled.

Y COLORIN COLORADO...

ESTE CUENTO SE HA ACABADO

The End

Glossary:

Doña: Mrs.

Cebolla: Onion

Rancho: Ranch

Tortilla: Tortilla

Chiles: Chili

Picantes: Spicy

Cilantro: Coriander

No se preocupe: Do not worry

Querida Amiga: My dear friend

Amigos: Friends

Se me ocurre algo: I have an idea

Bravo: Excellent

Y colorín colorado, este cuento se ha acabado: The End

Chilly Bolly Guacamolly's secret recipe for Guacamole:

Guacamole, a dip made from avocados, is originally from Mexico. The name is derived from two Aztec Nahuatl words - ahuacatl (avocado) and molli (sauce). The trick to perfect guacamole is using good, ripe avocados. Check for ripeness by gently pressing the outside of the avocado. If there is no give, the avocado is not ripe yet and will not taste good. If there is a little give, the avocado is ripe. If there is a lot of give, the avocado may be past ripe and not good. In this case, taste test first before using.

2 ripe avocados

red onion, minced (about 1/2 cup)

1-2 serrano chiles, stems and seeds removed, minced

2 tablespoons cilantro leaves, finely chopped

1 tablespoon of fresh lime or lemon juice

1/2 teaspoon coarse salt & a dash of freshly grated black pepper

1/2 ripe tomato, seeds and pulp removed, chopped

Smash all ingredients. Serve with tortilla chips. It is very IMPORTANT to be aware that by doing this the onion might make you cry.